Rudely awakened . . .

Kyle yawned. He thumped his pillow. He lay back down.

A huge shadow blotted out the light in his room.

For one uncomprehending moment, Kyle thought the curtains at his window had somehow blown shut.

Then he realized that the shadow was moving. Like a dark moon rising, it crept across the floor of his room, swallowing up all the still, small shadows in its darkness. It ate the shadow legs of the chair. Consumed the fat pear shadow of the lamp.

Only then did Kyle turn his head on his pillow, slowly, carefully, to look at his window.

A huge, round head, hard and white as a bowling ball, was pressed against the window. It had two glowing eyes, red and hot, like coals from the center of a red-hot fire. It had teeth of silver white, sharper than the blades of knives.

Kyle bolted upright. He opened his mouth. No sound came out. . . .

Other Skylark Books you won't want to miss!

GRAVEYARD SCHOOL

9

The Abominable Snow Monster

Tom B. Stone

A SKYLARK BOOK

Toronto   New York   London   Sydney   Auckland

RL 3.1, 008–012

THE ABOMINABLE SNOW MONSTER

A Skylark Book / November 1995

Skylark Books is a registered trademark of Bantam Books,
a division of Bantam Doubleday Dell Publishing Group, Inc.
Registered in U.S. Patent and Trademark Office and elsewhere.

Graveyard School is a trademark of
Bantam Doubleday Dell Publishing Group, Inc.

ISBN 0-553-48341-2

Published simultaneously in the United States and Canada

Bantam Books are published by Bantam Books, a division of Bantam
Doubleday Dell Publishing Group, Inc. Its trademark, consisting of the
words "Bantam Books" and the portrayal of a rooster, is Registered in
U.S. Patent and Trademark Office and in other countries. Marca
Registrada. Bantam Books, 1540 Broadway, New York, New York
10036.

PRINTED IN THE UNITED STATES OF AMERICA

0 9 8 7 6 5 4 3 2

GRAVEYARD SCHOOL

The Abominable
Snow Monster

CHAPTER
1

"What are you afraid of? Get out there and play!" Dr. Morthouse marched up behind the wad of students standing in the hall at the back door of Grove Hill Elementary School and threw open the door.

A blast of snow howled in.

"It's freezing out there," said Kyle Chilton. He pulled his ski mask down over his face so that only his eyes and mouth showed.

"Yeah," said Park Addams. "Like, you know—cold?"

Dr. Morthouse turned to face the sixth-graders huddled together for warmth in the hall behind her. "Cold?" she said. "*Cold?* You think this is cold? Ha! This is nothing. I used to walk miles to school in weather twice this cold."

"That's why the blood is frozen in your veins," muttered Stacey Carter, who was standing behind Kyle.

Dr. Morthouse's eyes narrowed, and everyone

shrank back. Then she smiled, and a silver glint flashed in her mouth.

Everyone shrank back even more.

"It's a fang," whispered Park. He was only half kidding.

"It's not a fang, it's an icicle," Stacey shot back.

Kyle might have laughed once. But he was too cold to laugh now. He was also afraid that if he opened his mouth and let in the cold air, he would freeze his teeth.

Dr. Morthouse was welcome to have icicle fangs. But Kyle wanted to keep his teeth as they were.

"The cold is good for you," Dr. Morthouse went on. "Builds character!"

It was afternoon recess at Grove Hill School, also known as Graveyard School. It was also late in the worst winter anyone in the town of Grove Hill could remember. Eleven major snowstorms had buried the town so far. This was the twelfth and meanest.

But Dr. Morthouse, principal of the school, wasn't about to let a little thing like a killer blizzard force her to close her school. Nor was she going to allow it to stop recess. She stepped back and said, "Now, go out and play. And have fun."

Numbly the students trooped out the door and into the snow.

The teachers followed their classes, but only as far as the top of the steps. They huddled there—shivering, miserable lumps. But they didn't go back inside. Dr. Morthouse was watching.

Most of the sixth-graders edged down the ice-clad steps and came to a halt in a frozen herd on the packed snow of the playground.

"We should keep moving," said Park. "If you stand still, you freeze."

"I'm too cold to move," wailed perfect Polly Hannah. For once she wasn't so perfect. Her baby-blue down jacket, with matching blue-and-pink-flowered scarf, mittens, and hat, had instantly become coated with ice and snow. Her nose was bright red and running.

But for once no one jumped at the chance to pay Polly back for past meannesses. They were all just as ice-encrusted and miserable.

Park bent over clumsily. He appeared to be wearing all the clothes he owned, and he looked like a big, down-stuffed red ball. He made a snowball.

"Don't you dare, Park!" shrieked Polly.

Park gave Polly a disgusted look. "I'm not gonna hit you with the snowball. I just thought maybe I could practice my pitching or something. Anybody wanna?"

No one did. Everyone moved closer together, stamping their feet and snorting like a herd of cattle. They stared balefully at Park.

"You're just going to freeze in one big lump," said Park. He tossed the snowball from one mittened hand to the other. "It happens, you know. Animals bunch up and think, *Ha, I'll keep warm with the other animals*, and they stop moving. The next day they're all frozen together like a big Jell-O mold."

"That's disgusting," Polly whined.

"It's true, though." Kyle spoke through stiff lips. His ski mask was sticking to his face.

Stacey reluctantly peeled herself away from the others. "You can throw it to me," she told Park. "But not hard."

Jaws Bennett, who boasted that he could eat almost anything, said, "Me too." He made a face. "I can eat frozen jelly beans, but what's the point? I think I'll wait until we go back inside and thaw them out."

Gradually the students began to spread out—slightly—across the playground. A few of the braver ones pried saucers and sleds from their ice-locked propping places and took them to the base of the hill at the end of the playground. A fence separated the lower part of the hill from the graveyard on the upper part.

The graveyard was what gave Grove Hill School its nickname—that and all the weird things that kept happening around the school. Strange, scary, horrible things that the adults didn't seem to notice, except maybe Mr. Bartholomew, also known as Basement Bart. Basement Bart was the school janitor, and he was pretty weird himself.

Some of the kids thought the old graveyard was the

cause of all the bizarre things that had happened. Some even said it was haunted and that there was a grave in it that glowed in the dark.

But no one knew for sure. No one ever hung out around the old graveyard, although a few kids, like Skate McGraw and his cousin, Vickie Wheilson, sometimes skateboarded on the steep, abandoned road at the top of Graveyard Hill. But strange things had happened to them, too. Things they wouldn't talk about.

In fact, Skate and Vickie were among the kids who were sledding. Kyle could hear Vickie complaining, characteristically, that the sled hill was a wimp slide. "Why can't we go sled the top of Graveyard Hill?" she said.

"Because," Kyle heard Skate answer. He knew what Skate meant: Because it's not part of the playground, and because the hill is steep, and because the teachers would say no, because that's what they're paid to say.

Skate was a person of few words.

"Great! We might as well play freeze tag," said Vickie in disgust.

"Puh-lease," he heard Maria Medina say.

Until someone spoke, Kyle wasn't always sure who was who under all the winter gear. Everyone looked as if they'd been inflated and let loose to bob across the playground in the wind and snow, winter versions of beach balls in their layers and layers of down and fiber-filled jackets, sweaters, snow pants, hats, scarves, mittens, and boots.

Hopping from one foot to the other, Kyle tried to remember the last time the sun had come out.

He couldn't.

Then he tried to imagine Dr. Morthouse as a child, trudging through the snow to school. But all he could picture was a shorter version of Dr. Morthouse now. He imagined her shoving mountains of snow aside with one arm, her schoolbooks tucked under the other like a quarterback with a football. The glint of her silver fang probably made the snow melt. . . .

No. Dr. Morthouse had never been a kid.

But Kyle still wished he could make her come stand in the snow. For hours. For days. He was sure it was much colder now than when she claimed she had been a kid. The greenhouse effect in reverse—not hotter but colder.

Yeah. That was it.

On the other hand, she would probably like it. The principal of Graveyard School wasn't human, after all. Everybody knew that.

"Kyle!" shouted Park.

Kyle ducked. A snowball shattered against his arm.

"Awww," said Stacey, "you killed the snowball."

"No problem," said Kyle bitterly. "There're plenty more where that came from." He hunched his shoulders and walked away.

"Well, excuuuuuuse me," said Stacey.

Kyle walked to the opposite corner of the school-yard, where the little kids played on seesaws and monkey bars and slides and swings. The white picket fence of the graveyard, almost entirely buried in snow, met the gray chain link of the school playground fence there, and the ground was so level that the snow was flat and smooth.

The half-buried playground equipment looked like the bones of dead animals, Kyle decided. Or dinosaurs. He dug his toe into the frozen snow and kicked. His boot made a perfect dent in the hard-packed surface. A faint spray of powder came up and was whipped away by the wind. He kicked again. And again.

The third time he kicked, his toe hit something hard. So hard that it gave his frozen toes a jolt, even through the boot.

"Owwwww!" He jumped back. Then he bent over.

He'd hit a rock. A hard, grimy, white, gray-veined rock. It looked like marble or polished granite, the same stone that was used in the cemetery above.

He kicked it again, trying to dislodge it. He must have kicked it harder than he realized, because a jolt of pain went up his leg.

"Uh," he said. He stepped back and knelt down and began to dig at the snow around the rock with his mittened hands. He scraped and dug, ignoring the tingling of his frozen fingers. At least he could still feel something, he reasoned. That meant he wasn't frozen solid. Yet.

He got his fingers under the rock and tried to pry it out. It barely moved. It was almost as if it were reluctant to leave its icy resting place.

Kyle forgot about the flurries of snow and the arctic wind and his deeply unhappy classmates shivering nearby. Suddenly he had to get the rock free. That was all that mattered.

He scraped and pried and scraped some more. Then he slid his whole mitten beneath one side of the cold lump of stone. He braced himself and yanked back.

The stone popped into the air, an ancient piece of marble as big as his fist. It turned end over end and then seemed to hang in front of his eyes for a moment, as if it were about to go into orbit.

Kyle jumped back. His mouth dropped open.

The stone fell with a heavy thud.

Unable to believe his eyes, Kyle bent forward to study the rock.

It was no ordinary rock. Someone had carved it once. Very realistically.

Kyle shuddered in spite of himself. Then he grinned and reached for his new treasure. He picked it up and held it at eye level in his mittened hand. It felt as if it weighed a ton. It covered his whole palm.

It was an enormous marble eyeball.

CHAPTER

2

"What is it?" asked a familiar, nosy voice.

Quickly Kyle shoved the eyeball in his pocket. "Nothing," he told Polly. "Aren't you supposed to be playing ball or something?"

"Why are you digging in the snow?" Polly asked, not giving up.

For some reason Kyle didn't want to tell Polly about the eyeball he'd found. What if she made him take it back to the graveyard? Obviously that was where it had been. But it was his now. Finders keepers.

He thought fast. "I'm digging in the snow because . . . because . . ." He looked around for inspiration and saw the ranks of crude snowmen that the little kids had built nearby. ". . . because I'm gonna build a snowman. Yeah, that's it. A snowman."

"A snowman?" Polly snorted. "That's so first grade! Besides, you'll get all messy."

Kyle could feel the weight of the monster-sized marble eyeball pulling at the pocket of his down parka. "Oh yeah? You're just saying that because you don't know how to build a decent snowman."

"Like I care!" Polly put her mitten-fattened hands on her down-swaddled hips and stomped her snow boot with an icy crunch.

A wild-pitch snowball came flying out of nowhere and skidded across the snow toward them. Kyle leaned forward and grabbed it. Then he began packing snow on it, making it bigger and bigger.

Stacey ran over. "Hey, that's our game ball," she said, only half joking.

"Not anymore," said Kyle. "Now it's the bottom of my snowman."

"Kyle's going to build one," said Polly scornfully. "Just like the little kids."

"Not just any snowman," said Kyle. He had forgotten that the whole idea had begun just to keep Polly from asking questions about the eyeball he'd found. But his mitten touched it now as he spoke and it seemed to give him added inspiration. "Not just any snowman," he repeated. "A snow *monster*."

Maria, Jaws, and Park had followed Stacey over. Now Park said, "A snow monster? Cool." Then he said, "Hey, I bet I could build a baseball player."

Maria said, "In your dreams. I'd build a snow-woman."

"A dog," said Stacey. She laughed. "Just like Morris." Morris was Stacey's bull terrier.

"Now, that would be a real monster. Morris-the-monster," Park cracked.

"I bet my monster could eat your baseball player," said Stacey.

"Not *my* baseball player," said Park. "I'm making Ty Cobb, the meanest baseball player who ever lived."

"This is all sooo stupid," said Polly.

Having given up on sledding, Maria had just come up to join the others. Now she gave Polly a look. "Why don't you go somewhere else and play?" she snapped. Maria had very little patience with Polly, even less than the rest of the kids. Not that Polly noticed. Polly never noticed anything unless it was something that could get another kid in trouble.

Polly sniffed. "Babies," she said to no one in particular, and turned and walked away.

Kyle gave her an evil look as she left. "When I finish my monster," he promised everyone, "the first thing he's gonna do is make snack food out of Polly."

A horn sounded from the end of the driveway that made a half-circle in front of the school. The sound was very distinctive: "Ah-*oooh*-gah! Ah-*oooh*-gah!"

· Kyle didn't cringe as he once had. He'd gotten over cringing long ago. Kyle's mother owned a garage with her father, Kyle's grandfather. Kyle's father was a musician. His mother liked to rig the car horn to play different tunes. Kyle's father supplied the tunes.

At the moment the car played what Kyle's father called the "old-movie car horn sound."

The other kids had gotten used to it, too, although Polly still took a shot at Kyle about it when she was around. Fortunately she wasn't around. Her mother had been the first to arrive, and they'd fishtailed away in the Hannahs' big gas-guzzling car almost before the final bell had stopped ringing.

"Aaah-*oooh*-gah!"

"My mom's here," Kyle said flatly to Stacey, Park, Maria, and Jaws.

They didn't usually carpool. They all lived close enough to walk or ride their bikes or, in Skate and Vickie's case, to ride their skateboards. But the bad weather had created winter car pools out of thin, cold air. Now, as Dr. Morthouse stood on the top steps by the front door, her arms folded and a scowl on her face, it was clear that it was the carpools of which she disapproved.

Wimps, she was clearly thinking. *You call this snow?*

Kyle's mother or father, whichever one was driving, always waved cheerfully to Dr. Morthouse. Kyle wasn't embarrassed by the dumb horn anymore, but he wasn't happy about that waving business. It was embarrassing *and* dangerous. Kids at Graveyard School never, *ever* voluntarily drew the principal's attention to themselves.

But nothing Kyle could say or do could persuade his parents to stop the practice. So he tried to sit in the backseat in the corner, in the hope that Dr. Morthouse would think he was someone else's kid.

Dr. Morthouse, of course, never waved back.

The horn "aah-*oooh*-gah'd" again and the five of them went down the stairs to meet the big red van as it pulled to a stop below.

"Hey, snowbunnies!" shouted Kyle's mother cheerfully.

Kyle groaned.

"Bunnies?" said Stacey to Kyle. *"Bunnies?"*

"How was your day?" she went on cheerfully as they piled quickly into the car.

"Fine, thank you," said Maria politely.

"Excellent," said Park. "We just chilled out all day, Mrs. Chilton. Chilled. Get it?"

"Got it, Parker. Very funny," said Kyle's mother.

They pulled away from the school. The wind was blowing harder now, and the snow whipped by in noisy gusts.

Kyle's mother leaned forward to peer through the front window. "I don't think this winter is *ever* going to end," she said as they inched down the snow-covered road. "I've never seen anything like it and I've lived here all my life. Twelve snowstorms in a row. Twelve! But who's counting?"

"My little sister fell off the back porch this weekend

and disappeared into a snowdrift," said Maria. "When my father jumped in to pull her out, the snow came up to his shoulders."

"She's lucky your father saw her," said Jaws solemnly. "She could have gotten trapped until the snow thawed. She'd have frozen to death. Or starved."

"If it happened to Morris, he'd probably try to eat his way out of the snowdrift," put in Stacey.

"Wow." Kyle turned to stare at Maria. The snow was melting on her dark, spiky bangs. "Was your sister mad?"

Maria grinned. "Nah, she thought it was fun," she told Kyle. "She wanted to do it again. Dad told her maybe later."

Mrs. Chilton let the others out, one by one, in front of their houses. She waited until they got up to their front doors. "So they don't get buried in any snowdrifts," she said.

At last it was just Mrs. Chilton and Kyle. Kyle moved to the front seat.

"Great day for ice cream, huh?" said his mother.

Kyle made a face. "Lame, Mom."

"You can take off your ski mask, you know. How can you see anything? Those eye holes would drive me crazy."

"How can *you* see anything?" answered Kyle. But he pulled off his ski mask. He'd forgotten he was wearing it.

"I can't see very much," his mother said. "But I'm pretty sure I'm not hitting anybody. And I'm almost definitely sure we're still on the road."

In Kyle's opinion, his mother had a very feeble, sick sense of humor. He suspected that it explained the whole horn business.

"It's supposed to stop sometime tonight," she went on. "And maybe it'll be the last one. After all, it's almost spring. Twelve snowstorms is enough for any year. Especially twelve snowstorms like these."

"I hope we have another one. A really, really big one," said Kyle.

"Thirteen? No. Sounds unlucky." His mother shook her head and put on the blinker. Peering through the front window, Kyle saw the mailbox at the foot of their driveway.

"Lucky," said Kyle. "Lucky thirteen, the biggest snowstorm of them all." Kyle thought of Dr. Morthouse standing by the back door of the school, telling them to go outside and play and have fun. "The kind that will close the school." His fingers touched the marble eyeball in his pocket and he smiled. "A monster snowstorm," he added.

But the snow stopped that night.

The next morning, for the first time in days, weeks, maybe months, the sun shined.

Park showed up at school wearing dark glasses.

"Snow-blind," he told everybody. "The reflection of the sun off the snow."

Dr. Morthouse made him take the glasses off in school. But Park wore them during recess. "They're for Ty Cobb when I finish," he explained, giving the pile of snow he'd been working on a pat.

Kyle concentrated on rolling the biggest snowball in the history of the school, so big that Maria and Park and Stacey had to help him push it to the base of the slide.

"The slide?" gasped Maria. "Why . . . way over here?"

"So . . . I can use . . . the ladder," panted Kyle.

They maneuvered the snowball into place and stepped back.

The base of the snow monster was almost as tall as Kyle. He liked that. Even though it was only a big, round ball of ice and snow, it already looked a little weird and scary—like the snowball from outer space, or something.

"Nice snowball," said Polly sarcastically. She came every recess to inspect the snow sculptures and offer criticism.

"I'm gonna use real body parts for the rest of it. You volunteering?" asked Kyle.

"You're disgusting," said Polly, and crunched away across the snow.

As the days passed and Kyle worked on his masterpiece, more and more students began to make snow sculptures. An army of snow figures grew up around the playground: a skateboard with a skeletal figure aboard it, a headless creature holding a bicycle helmet, a dinosaur with a foot dangling from its mouth, a family of werewolves.

Kids began to bring clothes and objects to decorate their creations. Park gave Ty Cobb an old baseball cap and bat and, of course, sunglasses. Stacey gave her snowdog, Morris, one of the real Morris's old collars and a dog-food dish. She even made him a snow bone.

The sun kept shining. No more snow fell. It didn't get warmer, but it didn't get any colder, either.

It took Kyle two days to roll the second ball of snow, which was almost as big as the first, up the slide and into place on top of the base of his snow monster.

The other kids finished their snow figures. Arguments broke out about whose was the best.

Kyle said, "You can't decide until I finish my monster. Besides, it's going to be the best."

"Nobody was better than Ty Cobb, the Georgia Peach," said Park. "Admit it."

"In person, he was the best," said Kyle. He looked down at Park's baseball player from the top of the slide and said, "But in snow, he's striking out, Park."

"Ty Cobb was a psycho, Park," said Stacey.

"He was a great ball player," said Park stubbornly.

"Just because you're good at something doesn't mean you get to act like a jerk," said Maria. "Look at

17

Wilma Rudolph, for example. She was a better athlete and a good person." Maria's snow figure had turned into the Olympic track star.

"You should have done Bonnie Blair, Maria," said Polly unexpectedly. "She won more Olympic medals than almost anybody. And that was for speed skating. A *winter* sport."

Kyle said, "My snow monster is going to be the best."

The days passed. The other kids drifted away to snow baseball and freeze tag and sledding. Kyle kept working. He finished the head. He rolled it up the slide.

It slid back down and broke into a million snowflakes. He started all over again.

The sun became his enemy. What if it got too warm? What if it melted his snow monster before he finished? He worked and worked and worked. He raced out the door the moment recess began, and he was the last one to race back inside. When Park pelted him with snowballs, Kyle ignored him. He refused to join the others in sledding or any of the other games.

He didn't have time for all that kid stuff.

"You're letting this take over your life," said Park, standing at the foot of the slide squinting up at Kyle. "You need to chill out."

"Ha," said Kyle. "Go away."

Park went away.

The little kids watched him with awe from a safe distance. But his classmates began to tease him. They sang

18

"Frosty the Snowman" when he walked by. They called him "ice cube head" and "snow brain."

No one understood why Kyle was so involved with his monster.

Kyle ignored them all. *They'll be sorry*, he thought, digging deeper and deeper into the snow, building the monster bigger and bigger. *They'll be sorry someday that they made fun of me.*

Someday soon.

He kept on working. Time was running out and he had a snow monster to finish.

And nothing was going to stop him.

CHAPTER

3

"Dah-dah-dah-dum."

Not one of his parents' more successful horn sounds, Kyle thought. His father said it was the opening notes of Beethoven's Fifth Symphony. Kyle had decided he never wanted to hear the rest. At least, not played on a car horn.

"Dah-dah-dah-*dum*."

Kyle raced for the kitchen door, then skidded to a stop. He frowned.

What was he forgetting?

He checked his pack: homework, books, notebooks. Then he remembered.

The eyeball. When he got home every afternoon, he took it out of his pocket and put it on his desk. It made a cool paperweight.

But today it was destined for greater things. Today was the day. His big day. The eyeball's big day.

The horn sounded a third time.

Kyle turned and made a mad dash for his room. He grabbed the eyeball off the desk.

It was so cold, he almost dropped it. Freezing! As cold as when he'd found it buried in the snow, even though he'd long since wiped off all the layers of ice and snow and dirt and gunk.

It had been pretty disgusting, he remembered. The gunk and dirt, mixed in with the melting snow and ice, had been almost like real eye goo. Or at least what he imagined real eye goo was like.

But now it was clean. And still as cold as ice.

Kyle put the eyeball down carefully and pulled on his glove. Then he picked up the marble carving again and lifted it as he had the first day he'd found it.

He stared at the eye and it stared back at him. It was perfectly round and worn smooth—no rough edges. Whatever statue it had fallen from in the old graveyard, it must have rolled downhill long, long ago to be worn so smooth.

Funny how the carving of the eye hadn't worn away, too. The eyelids and the eye itself were still perfectly clear. And very lifelike. He wondered what kind of statue in the old graveyard the eyeball could have come from.

The thought gave him a little chill.

Stop that, he told himself. *It's just marble. Cold, old, worn marble.*

Maybe the statue hadn't been human, he thought. It

didn't look like a human eyeball. He wondered if there were any statues of animals up on Graveyard Hill. He'd never seen any, but when he'd gone to his great-aunt's funeral, he'd seen all kinds of statues and tombstones in the cemetery in her hometown, where she'd been buried. Lambs. Angels. Shepherds. Even a carving of someone's pet dog.

He tossed the eyeball into the air and it spun around and landed neatly in his palm again.

"W-What?"

Kyle almost dropped it.

He blinked. It didn't.

It couldn't.

Must have been my imagination, he thought, stuffing it quickly in his pocket. He turned and hurried down to the car.

Yeah. My imagination. That's it. Because no way could that eyeball have winked.

No way on earth.

The bell rang.

The sixth-graders rose from their seats reluctantly. Slowly they began to put on the layers and layers of clothes they'd taken off when they'd arrived at school that morning. In a matter of minutes, the classroom was filled with kids who looked as if they'd been blown up with helium.

But they walked out the door into the hall as if they were dressed in lead suits.

"Recess!" said a self-satisfied, unnaturally cheerful voice. "You boys and girls are headed for recess!"

"Give the man an 'A,' " muttered Stacey to Kyle.

Hannibal Lucre, the assistant principal, bounded down the hall toward them. He was a short, round man who wore brown suits and combed one fat strand of brown hair across the bald spot on the top of his head. He was fond of telling the students, whenever he encountered them, "The principal is your pal. And the assistant principal, too. Ha, ha, ha."

No one had ever quite figured out a reply to that. The little kids mostly just fled without answering.

Park squinted up at Mr. Lucre from under the edge of his wool navy-surplus-store cap. "Yeah," he said in a muffled voice from behind the huge red-and-white-striped muffler wound around his neck and face. "Recess. Wanna come play with us?"

Mr. Lucre rubbed his plump hands together and laughed heartily.

As usual, he laughed alone.

"Thank you for your offer. . . . What an *impressive* and *unusual* sculpture garden you children have created on the playground. Most creative! No, no, I'll leave you children to go have a good time without me!"

"Yeah. If you can't stand the cold, stay out of the playground," said Stacey.

24

Mr. Lucre pretended not to hear. He walked bouncily away, still rubbing his hands together and talking to himself.

Too bad someone didn't freeze him when he was a kid, thought Kyle. *Or build a snowman and stick him in—permanently.*

Their teachers pushed the doors open. The cold air rushed in.

The students shuffled out.

Except for Kyle. Clutching his backpack, he shot through the doors and down the steps, headed for his snow monster.

Behind him he heard Polly whine, "It's gonna snow again. I just know it."

"Oh, go play with Mr. Lucre," he heard Maria snap.

Polly's voice went on. "My mother said the next snowstorm is probably going to be the worst snowstorm ever. She said we'll be lucky if we don't get buried alive. She said—"

"Could we stop talking about the weather?" asked Stacey.

Kyle heard them crunching along behind him as he dropped his pack in the snow by the slide. He climbed up the ladder.

When he reached the top rung, he realized that he could barely see over the huge white ball of snow that was his monster's head. His monster towered over the other snowmen. It towered over everything in the

25

schoolyard. It even towered over the statues in the graveyard.

It was a monster-sized monster. Kyle began to smooth the rough spots on the huge head carefully, proudly.

Below, footsteps crunched to a stop. Polly said, "So it's big. So what. A big, ugly snowman. It doesn't even have a face."

"Stand still, Polly," said Kyle without turning around. "I'll copy your face onto it."

Maria and Stacey and the other kids snickered.

"Good one," said Park. Then he said, "You know, maybe you should take a break. You've been working on that thing for days. Too much hard work can kill a person, you know."

Jaws, who was chewing a wad of bubble gum, started to blow a bubble, then thought better of it. "Yeah," he said gummily. "It's not healthy."

"See? Even Jaws agrees. You need to take a break from that snowman."

"Snow monster," said Kyle.

Park shook his head. "Whatever."

The monster's head was as hard and as smooth as a bowling ball now, but ten times bigger. Kyle took a small water pistol out of his inside pocket and squirted the icy surface. He quickly smoothed it even more before the water froze.

He looked down. Maria and Stacey and Polly and the

others had wandered off. But Park and Jaws were still watching him.

"Later," said Kyle firmly.

Park and Jaws exchanged looks. Park shrugged. Jaws chewed. They turned and walked away.

Kyle was alone with his creation.

He lost track of time as he sprayed and patted and made sure that all the surfaces were perfectly smooth, perfectly round. The weak gray shadows cast by the fading winter sun shortened.

At last Kyle climbed back down the ladder. He snagged his pack and dragged it back up to the top of the slide.

Opening the pack, Kyle peered inside thoughtfully. He'd brought a number of objects to use for eyes and nose and mouth. But they all seemed so ordinary. At last he decided on his collection of fake shark teeth. Using his water pistol and his numb fingers, he cut a wide, wicked grin in the front of the monster's head. He inserted the shark teeth.

The big head looked gruesome now, a blank surface with an evil grin, like the man in the moon gone berserk.

Kyle liked that.

He went back down the ladder and gave the snow monster a big smile. He wondered what it would be like to have shark teeth.

Kyle scouted around under the frozen, skeletal trees at the edge of the playground and found two gnarled and knobby branches. He climbed back up the ladder and stuck the branches into the second ball where the shoulders would be.

Now the snow monster had arms and hands.

Kyle went back to the snow monster's blindly smiling head. He scooped out two eye sockets. Then, reaching into his pocket, he took out the marble eyeball and carefully stuck it into the left socket.

It was gross. One empty socket, one stone eyeball.

It was perfect.

Kyle leaned on the top of the slide and folded his arms with satisfaction. He looked around the playground. The other things made of snow, the people and animals, decorated with old hats and scarves and collars, with their plastic buttons and their carrot and potato noses and radish eyes, all looked silly in comparison. Puny.

"Ha," said Kyle.

Something hit him in the stomach.

"Wha—!"

It hit him again.

With a terrible shriek, Kyle fell backward, all the way down the slide.

He was buried alive, just like Maria's little sister. He couldn't get out. He was stuck headfirst in the snow and he couldn't get out.

He was going to drown in snow. Smother in it. He was—

"Hey! Watch it!" a voice complained.

Hands caught his ankles and dragged him upright.

Sputtering and shivering, Kyle began to brush the snow away from his head and neck. "Th-Thanks," he said through chattering teeth.

Park looked around at the collection of lower-graders who had gathered. "This is a move only professionals should try," he said. "Do not try it on your own."

"Oh, brother," said Jaws.

The little kids just stared.

They stared at Kyle. Then they stared at the snow monster. Their nervous gazes flicked back and forth.

"What happened?" said Park. "We looked over and you'd taken a header right off the slide."

Kyle frowned. He remembered something hitting him in the stomach. But what?

He looked up. A small chill snaked down his spine, and not from the melting snow under the collar of his jacket.

His snow monster towered above them. But one of its arms had moved.

No way, thought Kyle.

"The wind," he said aloud. "The wind caught one of the snow monster's arms and it hit me and knocked me off balance."

To Kyle's ears the explanation sounded pretty puny. But everybody else seemed to accept it.

Park was nodding, staring up at the monster, too. "Decent," he said. "In fact, awesome."

Murmurs of admiration and praise rose from the others. Kyle smiled proudly, forgetting his stupid tumble. He'd done it. He'd created a monster.

CHAPTER
4

The wind howled. It grew darker. And darker.

And darker still where the giant shadow fell across the frozen snow.

Kyle shivered. He sat up in bed.

He'd just had a bad dream. A dream about snow. About . . .

His eyebrows drew together and he frowned, trying to remember. But he couldn't.

Looking around the room, he realized that although it was very, very late, he could see everything clearly. The blanket of snow that covered Grove Hill, like snow everywhere, was a great reflector of light. The least bit of light bounced off it and illuminated the world. Especially, thought Kyle, when it was nearly time for a full moon.

When the full moon came, he'd be able to do his homework by the reflection from the snow.

Not that he'd be doing his homework . . .

It was almost bright enough tonight to read by. The light reflecting through the window cast shadows across the room: spidery shadow legs from his desk chair, a pear-shaped shadow from his lamp.

Late and quiet and still. Maybe it was the absolute stillness that had awakened him. For once the wind wasn't howling through the twisted, frozen branches of the trees. For once it wasn't shrieking down the streets and wailing at the windows, trying to drive the snow in through the glass itself.

For once the winter night was peaceful and calm and silent.

Kyle yawned. He thumped his pillow. He lay back down.

A huge shadow blotted out the light in his room.

For one uncomprehending moment, Kyle thought the curtains at his window had somehow blown shut.

Then he realized that the shadow was moving. Like a dark moon rising, it crept across the floor of his room, swallowing up all the still, small shadows in its darkness. It ate the shadow legs of the chair. Consumed the fat pear shadow of the lamp.

Only then did Kyle turn his head on his pillow, slowly, carefully, to look at his window.

A huge, round white head, hard and white as a bowling ball, was pressed against the window. It had two glowing eyes, red and hot, like coals from the center of a red-hot fire. It had teeth of silver white, sharper than the blades of knives.

Kyle bolted upright. He opened his mouth. No sound came out.

The head turned. The red coal eyes fastened on Kyle.

The snow monster grinned, and the teeth glittered with an evil light of their own. Then one black tree-bone hand came up and scratched softly at the window.

"Nooooooooo!" screamed Kyle. *"Nooooooo!"*

He was still screaming when the lights went on.

"Kyle! Son! What is it?" The door of Kyle's room crashed open and Kyle's father ran in, his bathrobe flapping around his legs, his glasses clutched in one hand.

"Noooo-ooo. . . ." Kyle's voice trailed off. He looked wildly at his father, then back at the window. He raised a shaking hand and pointed.

"Wind—wind—it was at the window," he stuttered.

Mr. Chilton crossed the room and peered out Kyle's window. Then he remembered his glasses and put them on and peered out again.

"Nothing there now," he said in a hearty, jovial, humor-the-scared-kid voice. "Not a thing—except a little snow."

"Snow." Kyle's voice squeaked. "A snowman. I mean, monster. It was—"

"A bad dream," said his father firmly. He turned to look at Kyle. Nearsighted blue eyes met wide, frightened ones.

33

Then Kyle blinked. He looked away from his father at the window. It was just a dark square.

"Maybe it was the wind," said his father. "Woke you up. Happens to me sometimes."

There is no wind, thought Kyle. Couldn't his father hear? The silence—except for his own ragged breathing and his father's jovial voice—was the only sound.

Slowly Kyle nodded. "Right, Dad," he said, trying to make his voice sound normal and, to his amazement, more or less succeeding. "The wind."

"We were supposed to get some more snow," said his father, glancing back out the window, "but it looks like it's holding off a little while longer. It's actually kind of a nice night. Except for the freezing cold and the snow."

"Yeah," said Kyle. He lay back down and pulled the covers up. "Sorry about that, Dad."

"No problem." His father patted the covers above Kyle's feet. "Want anything? Water? Want me to leave the light on?"

"Nah." His father turned to go, but Kyle said suddenly, "Dad?"

His father turned with an inquiring look.

"Before you go, would you close the curtains?"

As his father left, Kyle kept his eyes on the now closed curtains. The lights went out. Every muscle in Kyle's body tensed.

But nothing happened.

Maybe it was a nightmare, thought Kyle. *A dumb, little-kid nightmare.*

He waited some more.

And still nothing happened.

Had to be, he thought, his eyelids growing heavy. *Had to be a bad dream. Hah, Kyle, you big dummy. The next thing you know, you'll start thinking there are things hiding under the bed. Hanging out in the closet. Just waiting for you to turn out the lights.*

Grow up. Get a grip. What are you—a little kid or a sixth-grader?

Kyle yawned. He closed his eyes. He fell asleep.

The room stayed quiet and dark.

The night outside stayed bright. And still. No wind. No snow.

Just the occasional shudder of the frozen, snow-coated earth as something huge passed over it.

"My snowmaaaaan!" a little kid began to wail.

"Hey! What happened to Morris the snow dog?"

"At least Ty Cobb put up a fight," wisecracked Park.

The wails of other little kids split the air.

Kyle stopped walking toward his snow monster. He stared at the carnage around him. Sometime between the end of school the day before and now, someone had gone through the playground and really kicked some snow. Big-time.

Snow people and animals had been chopped in half, stomped to pieces, decapitated. Morris the snow dog was a pile of lumpy snow, except for his dog dish, which was turned upside down on what once might have been his head.

Ty Cobb was facedown in the snow. His baseball bat was lying across the backs of his knees.

Potato and carrot noses and radish eyes were scattered across trampled snow, along with hats and scarves and shoes and buttons, like some big, crazy salad.

It was creepy.

"This is so mean!" said Maria, putting her hands where her hips would have been if she hadn't been wearing dozens of layers of clothes to stay warm.

"Sick," said Park. He shook his head.

"What a mess," said Polly in a voice that sounded full of deep satisfaction.

Everyone turned to look at her.

"What?" said Polly. "What?" Then she said, "Why are you all looking at me? I didn't do it!"

"Who said you did?" asked Stacey, narrowing her eyes.

"I wouldn't do something like this," said Polly indignantly.

Maria shook her head. "Probably not," she said, her voice tinged with what could have been regret.

Now it was Polly's turn to narrow her eyes and put her hands on her hips.

The two girls faced each other.

"Fight, fight, fight!" chanted Park, and he and Jaws pretended to leap back out of the way.

But Kyle wasn't watching. He was staring at his snow monster.

A dream. A nightmare.

His monster was untouched. Intact. Just the way he'd left it. Standing, no, looming in the corner of the playground.

Its empty eye socket looked coldly out at nothing. Its marble eye peered down at the pitiful humans and crushed snow sculptures below. Its stick arms stuck stiffly out from its rounded shoulders. The teeth grinned.

But now it was wearing a top hat.

"Hey!" screeched one of the little kids. "That's my hat! The hat I had on my snowman!"

His voice was loud and piercing. Everyone on the playground turned to look at him. Then they all turned to look where he was pointing.

Polly, of course, was the first to speak.

"How come nothing happened to *your* snowman, Kyle?"

Her shrill whine was just as penetrating as the little kid's screech. Everyone turned from the snow monster to look at Kyle.

Kyle swallowed nervously. What was the answer? He opened his mouth.

A cloud blotted out the sun. An ugly gray shadow swallowed up the whole playground. A gust of wind howled down off Graveyard Hill.

"The wind," said Kyle. "The wind is what blew everything to pieces. My snow mon—snowman—didn't get trashed because it's over there in the corner. It was protected. Also, I'd sprayed it with water, so it had an ice coating. That made it extra-strong, see?"

Polly said, "Then how did the little kid's hat get on its head?"

Before Kyle could answer, the little kid said indignantly, "That's my hat!" He ran across the playground and began to scramble up the ladder.

Kyle leaped forward. Some instinct made him shout, "No! Wait!"

But he was too late. Just as the little kid reached the top of the ladder, another icy gust of wind tore down the hill. Everyone clutched at their coats and hats.

Everyone except Kyle. He was struggling across the ice toward his snow monster. His eyes were fixed on the little kid, who looked like a puffy ant and who was reaching for the top hat.

As Kyle watched, one of the stick arms swept up viciously and caught the little kid right between the shoulders.

"Ugh!" the little kid said, and skidded headfirst down the ice-coated slide.

Kyle reached him first. "Hey! Are you okay?" The

kid had landed hands- and headfirst in the drift of snow that covered the bottom half of the slide. Kyle caught him by the back of his jacket and hauled him off the slide and through the drift.

"Hey!" said the little kid. "Let me go! Put me down!"

Kyle put him down, and the kid immediately sank up to his waist. He struggled out of the drift to the hard-packed, trampled snow next to Kyle and looked up at Kyle accusingly, wiping the snow out of his eyes.

"I want my hat back," said the little kid.

"You aren't hurt?" asked Kyle.

"No." The kid paused, scowling. He was a tough-looking little kid, with thick, straight, black eyebrows that were so close together, they probably made him look as if he were scowling even when he wasn't. Then he said, "How did you do that?"

"Do what?" asked Park. Kyle looked up and realized that the other kids were gathering around them.

"Knock me down from the slide so I couldn't get my hat."

Kyle forced himself to laugh, even though his heart was pounding. He was afraid to look at his snow monster. "I didn't knock you down. The wind blew you off balance and you fell. Same thing happened to me the other day. You have to be careful. Those steps on the slide are icy."

The kid scowled harder. "I felt you. I felt you *push* me."

To Kyle's surprise, it was Polly who came to his rescue, even though she didn't mean to. She gave the little kid a look of complete, withering scorn and said, "Oh, grow up. He didn't push you. How could he have?"

The little kid looked confused. Then his face began to crumple. He wasn't so tough after all. "I want my hat!" he wailed. "I want my hat!"

"Okay, okay, I'll get your hat," said Kyle quickly.

Jaws leaned forward and gave the little kid a thump on the shoulder. The kid staggered slightly. Jaws was strong. "There," said Jaws. "He's gonna get your hat. Lighten up."

The little kid sniffled. But he stopped. He folded his arms and stuck out his lower lip and glared at Kyle.

Little phony, thought Kyle. *There aren't any tears in his eyes!*

But what could he do? It was the little kid's hat. *No big deal,* he told himself. He'd just climb up the ladder and get it.

Without looking up at his snow monster, Kyle walked around the slide and began to climb the ladder. His heart began to pound harder than ever.

Don't be silly, he told himself. *You were just imagining things. Your snow monster is just an oversized snowman with bad teeth. That's it. Nothing's going to happen. Nothing.*

What could happen?

Even as he asked himself the question, Kyle had a

sudden vision of the snowman turning and reaching out with its bone-branch arms, fastening the twisted claw-branch hands on Kyle, lifting him up, and opening its big, shark-toothed mouth wide.

Kyle had reached the top of the ladder.

"My hat," said the kid in his thin, sharp voice.

Kyle looked at the snowman and then looked quickly away. He looked down at the crowd below.

A tiny swirl of wind blew past. The arms moved slightly, slightly.

Kyle took a deep breath and reached for the hat.

CHAPTER
5

Nothing happened.

The hat came off in Kyle's hands.

Holding it carefully, Kyle backed down the ladder. He walked over and thrust the hat into the kid's outstretched mittens. "Here."

With the hat clutched in both hands, the kid took off.

"Good save, Kyle," said Park with cheerful sarcasm.

Stacey said, "What I don't understand, though, is how the hat stayed on in that wind."

"What *I* don't understand," said Polly, "is how the hat got there in the first place. You can't say the wind did that, can you, Kyle?" She widened her pale blue eyes and tried to look surprised instead of as if she wanted to cause trouble.

Stacey's green eyes narrowed. "True."

Kyle thought fast. He folded his arms. "Are you saying *you* did it, Polly?" he asked. "Because that's what it sounds like."

"Me?" Polly's voice went up. *"Me?"*

Park said thoughtfully, "You were the one who noticed that Kyle's snowman wasn't trashed. And you were the one who noticed that the hat stayed on. It's like you wanted us to suspect Kyle."

"Yeah," said Kyle.

Her green eyes still narrow, Stacey nodded. "True," she said again.

"I didn't do anything to anybody's stupid snowman. It was Kyle!"

"Yeah, right, Polly," said Kyle. "I snuck over here in the middle of the night and beat up all the snowmen on the playground. Except my own."

"That is what you did, isn't it," said Polly.

"No!" said Kyle.

"I say it is," said Polly. "Quit trying to make *me* look guilty!"

She put her hands on her hips and leaned forward. Keeping his arms folded, Kyle leaned forward, too. They glared at each other.

Finally Polly said, "Eat snow and die, Kyle Chilton." She turned and stomped off.

As she crossed the playground, she paused for a moment to glare at some first-graders who were busily reconstructing their snowman. The first-graders shrank back.

"Take that!" said Polly, and gave the snowman a vicious kick.

Wow, thought Kyle. *If I didn't know better, I'd think Polly really did it.*

"I didn't think even Polly had it in her," Maria murmured.

Feeling guilty, Kyle said, "Maybe she didn't—"

He stopped as everyone turned to stare at him.

"—have a good day and that's why she did it," he finished weakly.

"And maybe she didn't do it at all," said Park softly, giving Kyle a funny look.

"I didn't do it," said Kyle.

"Maybe you did and maybe you didn't," said Park. He looked up at the snow monster. He looked back at Kyle.

Suddenly Maria shivered. "It's getting colder," she said. "It feels like it's going to—"

Before she even finished her sentence, big, fat flakes of snow began to drift down from the sky.

"—snow," said Maria glumly.

The flakes began to fall faster and faster.

"The thirteenth snowstorm," said Kyle softly.

No one answered.

The bell for the end of recess rang.

Still not speaking, everyone turned to troop back into the school.

At the top of the back steps, Kyle turned to look out through the thick rain of flakes. The tumbled, trampled,

45

crushed figures made of snow looked like distorted copies of the ancient, worn tombstones on the hill above the school. It was creepy.

But not half so creepy as Kyle's monster, standing watch from the corner of the playground.

The snow fell for the rest of the day, heavier and heavier. Faster and faster. The wind moaned and plucked at the windows and doors, and at the nerves of the inhabitants of Graveyard School.

All except Kyle. He hardly noticed except when he looked out the window and felt a sense of relief mixed with dread as he realized that the heavy snow made the world outside the windows invisible: no graveyard up on the hill, no playground.

No huge white snow monster standing watch.

And waiting to come to life.

It can't be true, thought Kyle, staring at the white wall of snow outside the classroom window. *It's scientifically impossible. It's just science fiction, like that book* Frankenstein, *where Dr. Frankenstein built that monster and it came to life. That didn't happen.*

And this isn't happening either. I didn't build a snow monster. It's crazy to think I could.

I'm not *Dr. Frankenflake.*

Something tapped on the window near his desk, and he jumped a mile. A tattered leaf that had somehow survived the winter storms clung there for a moment longer, like a hand pressed against the window begging to be let in. Then it tore loose and disappeared into the storm.

Kyle put his own hands to his face.

No such thing as a monster, he told himself.

"Are you listening? Kyle?"

Kyle put down his hands. He stared up at his teacher dully.

"Kyle, are you listening to what I'm saying?"

No such thing as a monster.

"Yes," said Kyle.

But deep inside he knew he wasn't listening. Not to his teacher. Not to himself.

Because there was such a thing as a monster. He'd created one out of snow and ice and branches and plastic teeth.

And the terrible eyeball that must have come from up on Graveyard Hill.

The sound of the horn barely pierced the thick curtain of snow.

"Isn't that your car, Kyle? Kyle?"

Park nudged Kyle. Kyle shook his head.

The entire school was packed on the top steps and pressed against the front doors of Graveyard School, trying to stay out of the wind and the snow that had begun to beat mercilessly down. Only two people weren't in danger of being crushed by the mass of students seeking shelter from the storm while they waited for the bus or for their rides home from school:

Dr. Morthouse, who was standing in the middle of the top of the stairs like the spooky figurehead of some old ship, her coat thrown open, her face turned into the wind, as if by glaring at it she could make it stop.

And Kyle. The little kids were giving him a wide berth. Kyle the hat thief. Kyle the snowman-killer. Kyle the monster-builder who pushed little kids off slides and maybe worse.

The other sixth-graders weren't exactly avoiding Kyle, but they were giving him looks. Polly was clearly talking about him, glancing over toward him as she whispered behind her pastel mittens. And Park had given Kyle more than one puzzled look and several times had seemed about to speak, to ask Kyle a question. But each time, he'd stopped.

As if he didn't really want to know the answer.

Kyle kept brooding.

"It *is* our ride," said Maria, blowing on her mittened fingers. "Kyle, that's your car, isn't it?"

"Yeah," said Kyle. Maybe the snowstorm would bury his monster, he was thinking. Bury it alive.

Or maybe they'd have a sudden heat wave and—

"Come on!" shouted Stacey. "Before we freeze!" She charged down the steps, and the others charged after her.

Barely realizing what he was doing, Kyle allowed himself to be pulled along with Stacey and Park and Jaws and Maria.

Halfway down the stairs, the wind caught Park's red-and-white-striped scarf and whipped it into the air.

"Hey!" Park made a grab and almost fell. Jaws grabbed Park, and both of them lurched into Kyle. The three of them slipped and stumbled and crashed to the bottom of the stairs.

As they got to their feet, Kyle thought he heard the sound of laughter. Shrill, gleeful, nasty laughter.

He turned to glare in the direction where he'd last seen Polly.

Then he made a dive for the car.

His mother was hunched over the steering wheel, wrapped in what looked like all the winter clothes she owned.

Everyone said hello with breathless politeness.

Mrs. Chilton said, "Close the door. Quickly!" They'd barely had time to obey before she was pulling away from the curb with a jerk.

"They should have closed school early," said Kyle's mother grumpily. "This is ridiculous."

"Tell that to Dr. Morthouse," offered Kyle.

"Maybe I will," said Mrs. Chilton. They reached a stop sign, and the car skidded slightly.

"Does this car have, like, you know, four-wheel drive?" asked Jaws.

"Yeah," said Kyle. "All our cars do."

"All your cars?" said Jaws.

"Jaws, my family owns a garage," said Kyle.

"Oh, yeah, right," said Jaws.

Kyle's mother said, "Four-wheel drive *and* snow tires. But I wonder if I shouldn't have put on snow chains. . . ." The car skidded again slightly, then straightened out, and they drove on.

"This is amazing," said Stacey, rubbing her arm along the window, trying to see out.

Kyle looked toward the playground. Nothing. Blinding white and nothing more.

"Quit breathing, you guys. You're fogging up the windows," said Kyle's mother, only half kidding. She bent forward even more, so that her nose seemed about to touch the front window. "It's funny," she murmured. "It wasn't this bad when I got to the school."

They inched onward.

Park said, "I guess even your snow monster's gonna be eating snow on this one, huh, Kyle."

Kyle shrugged.

"This is gonna wipe out the whole playground. I bet even the swings get buried. Maybe even the school," said Maria enthusiastically.

"I wouldn't be surprised," muttered Mrs. Chilton.

"And Dr. Morthouse will close the school!" concluded Stacey triumphantly. "Hey, maybe this isn't such a bad snowstorm after all."

Maybe it wasn't, thought Kyle, suddenly feeling fractionally more cheerful. Maybe it would bury the monster. Maybe it was only his imagination after all. A night of bad dreams, a day of bad wind and snow—that's all it was. Just a string of coincidences and bad luck.

He leaned back. He began to relax.

Something rocked the car so hard that the wheels lifted off the ground on one side and then the other.

Mrs. Chilton stomped on the brakes. "Whoaaaaaa!" she said.

"Good grief!" said Stacey. "Was that the wind?"

"Awesome!" exclaimed Park.

"Awful, you mean," said Maria.

Mrs. Chilton wrenched the wheel around. "I've never felt wind like this," she confessed. "It felt like a small tornado."

Abruptly the car rocked again. This time it seemed to fishtail, swinging wildly from one side to the other.

Jaws, who'd been sitting in the front seat and wearing his seat belt, held on to the dashboard. In the backseat the four of them were thrown from side to side. Mrs. Chilton, who was also wearing her seat belt, hung on to the wheel grimly.

As quickly as it had begun to rock and skid, the car straightened out.

"Put on your seat belts back there. Now!" snapped Mrs. Chilton.

No one argued.

"Are we almost home?" asked Jaws.

Kyle's mother didn't answer. She drove slowly, slowly forward.

"Mom? Where are we? Are we almost home?" asked Kyle.

Without taking her eyes from the blinding snow outside the car, Kyle's mother said, "I don't know. I don't know where we are."

CHAPTER
6

"We're lost?" said Kyle. "Mom, cut it out. This is not funny."

"I'm not trying to be funny," his mother said grimly. Then she said, "But it's not an emergency. We're still on the road. We're still moving. As soon as we get to a house, we'll pull up and wait for the storm to be over."

No one spoke.

Then Maria said, "Yeah. That'll be cool. Like in this book I read about these guys who got trapped in a blizzard? Well, they stopped in their car, see, and the snowplows didn't see them? And they ran right over them!"

"Thanks for sharing, Maria," said Stacey, rolling her eyes.

Jaws said, "Are we gonna miss dinner?"

Park said to Jaws, "You're kidding, right?"

Jaws frowned.

Another gust of wind hit the car, this time from behind. It shot forward and spun wildly.

Everyone began to scream. Park threw up his arms. Jaws dove sideways in his seat. Maria and Stacey grabbed each other and closed their eyes.

Kyle didn't scream. He didn't close his eyes. He was too scared.

Because he'd seen something out his window, right as the blast of wind had hit. Something dark and clawlike. Something branchlike but horribly alive.

A hand. A tree-branch hand, like blackened bone, but grown now. Bigger. More clawlike.

He'd seen, pressed against one side of the car, the fingers splaying down across the top of the window, curling, clutching.

Pushing.

It wasn't the wind that was pushing the car.

It was something much, much worse. Something alive.

It was the monster.

The car skidded to a crashing halt. There was the sound of something breaking.

A gust of wind whipped through the car, and then everything was still.

Somewhere in the corner of his mind Kyle had a moment of admiration for his mother. She hadn't screamed. She hadn't panicked.

Kyle turned his head slowly and stared forward. The

front window was smashed in. The safety glass was already being blown away in crumbly chunks by the howling wind.

It was freezing in the car.

"Where are we?" asked Maria, her voice slightly shaky. "What happened?"

"We must have hit a bad patch of ice right as a gust of wind caught us," said Mrs. Chilton. To Kyle's relief, she sounded completely calm and in control.

"We've stopped," said Park. Kyle could tell that Park was trying to sound calm and in control, too. But Park's voice was definitely as shaky as Maria's. "The window's broken."

"Looks like a branch went through it," said Kyle's mother.

Stacey said, "Wow! That wind just picked us up like a dog picks up a toy. Amazing."

Stacey sounded as calm as Kyle's mother.

Jaws moved his lips, but no sound came out.

"We're not moving," said Maria. She had to raise her voice to be heard above the scream of the wind. "Are we still on the road?"

Mrs. Chilton didn't answer Maria directly. Instead she said, "I think we hit something besides that branch."

She put her hand on the door handle.

Kyle found his voice at last. "Hey!" he said. "Hey, Mom! You're not going out there!"

His mother looked over her shoulder at Kyle in surprise. "I'm not going to leave you," she said reassuringly.

"You could get lost in this weather. Like in those books about the pioneers going out to milk their cows in the barns and being found frozen halfway between the barn and the house because they got lost," said Kyle.

Mrs. Chilton raised her eyebrows. "I know, Kyle. I'm going to go take the emergency kit out of the trunk. I'm going to put one flare by the car and I'm going to tie the rope to the door handle and hold on to it while I check this out. Okay?"

"It'll be okay, Kyle," said Stacey reassuringly. "Your mom knows what she's doing."

Kyle swallowed hard. What could he say? "Be careful, there's a snow monster out there?" "I think the storm made it grow?" "I think it wants to eat people?" "I think it might eat you?"

"Don't go," he said at last in desperation, aware that he sounded like a big wimp baby.

"I'll be right back," said his mother, and smiled. "Stay close together and try to keep warm. I'll bring some blankets from the trunk."

She slid out of the car and closed the door. They listened as the trunk opened. A few minutes later the faint light of the flare appeared by the car and they saw the dim outline of Mrs. Chilton's red down parka. She opened the door and tossed in two sleeping bags and a blanket. "Here," she said. "The bags unzip to make blankets. Wrap yourselves up."

She closed the door. The five of them wrapped themselves in the blanket and sleeping bags as Mrs. Chilton tied the rope to the door handle. She waved at them and held up her end of the rope. Then she walked forward and disappeared into the storm.

Kyle looked wildly around, straining to see. He knew the monster was out there. Was it waiting? Was it about to grab his mother?

A gust of wind shook the car.

Kyle leaped up in his seat. "Noooo!" he gasped.

"Chill, Kyleman. Just the wind," said Park, giving Kyle a funny look.

Kyle realized that this time it was indeed just the wind. He slumped in his seat. But he could feel his eyes rolling wildly in his head.

What was taking his mom so long? What if she'd dropped the rope?

What if the rope broke?

What if something came along and bit it into two pieces?

Kyle had a sudden, sickening vision of a fishing trip to nearby Slime Lake one summer when he was younger. He'd pulled and pulled on his fishing line. Suddenly it had come flying up in the air.

Nothing was on the end of it: no bait, no hook, no

cork, no sinker. Something had bitten the whole end of his fishing line off.

"Must have been a big one. A monster fish," he could hear his father saying.

Those big teeth. Big, stupid plastic shark teeth. Except bigger now. And probably not exactly made of plastic anymore . . .

No, thought Kyle. He lunged for the door handle.

Something loomed up in the window.

"Aaah!" shrieked Kyle before he could stop himself.

The car door opened and his mother slid back inside, coated with snow like a big, red, weird, sugar-coated doughnut.

"Whew!" she said. "That is the worst storm I have ever been in."

"This is not good news," said Park. He'd regained some of his old cocky attitude, almost as if Kyle's wimping out had given him strength.

I have to pull myself together, thought Kyle. He took a deep breath.

In the front seat his mother went on, "Maybe not, Park. But I do have some good news. We're in the Banks."

"This is good news?" asked Stacey. The Banks (called the Moneybanks by most of Grove Hill) was the rich people's section of the town. The houses were all huge and miles apart and miles from the road.

"Well, yes, it is," said Mrs. Chilton with a little laugh.

"What we hit was the front gate. I know whose house this is—Mr. King's. He uses our garage for all his cars. There's a fence that goes all the way up the drive because there's a pasture on one side. I can follow the fence up to the house and get help."

"Bad idea, Mom," said Kyle. "You're not supposed to leave the car in a snowstorm."

"We can't stay here," answered Kyle's mother. "The whole front window's broken. We'll freeze to death."

Or be eaten alive, thought Kyle. *Frozen dinners.*

"Mom," he said.

She held up her hand. "Kyle, it'll be all right. Jaws, get in the backseat. I want you all to get under the sleeping bags and stay there until I get back with help. Don't get out of the car for any reason. Don't get separated. If you stay under the sleeping bags and blankets and huddle together for warmth, you should be all right until I return."

"Do you want one of us to go with you?" asked Stacey.

"Stay here!" said Mrs. Chilton almost sharply. "Here are some flares and the emergency supply kit. If you hear anyone coming, light the flares." She smiled at Maria. "That should prevent the snowplows from hitting you, although I don't think that's a problem. They'd be moving very slowly. Meanwhile I'll be back as soon as I can."

With a reassuring nod, she slid out of the car and slammed the door.

They watched her go. All too quickly she disappeared into the snowstorm.

They were alone.

Alone with the monster, thought Kyle.

"We could zip the two sleeping bags together to make one big sleeping bag," suggested Maria.

"There are five of us," Park pointed out. "Two sleeping bags, five people. We won't fit."

"We might," said Maria. "These are adult sleeping bags."

"Let's just pull them over us and try to make a kind of tent," said Stacey.

A blast of snow swept into the car.

"Like immediately," she added. "Like *now.*"

They scrambled under the sleeping bags and pulled them up over their heads.

"Is there any trail mix in that emergency kit?" asked Jaws hopefully.

"No," said Park. "We're not eating anything yet. We're saving it for an emergency."

"This is an emergency, Park. In case you hadn't noticed," said Jaws.

"Not yet," said Park. "No food yet."

Silence fell. Jaws got out his headphones and turned on the music.

Maria grimaced and huddled deeper into her clothes beneath the shadowy tent of the blankets.

No one spoke. The wind howled. Kyle strained to hear anything above that sound. But he couldn't. After a while, in spite of himself, his muscles began to relax.

He was so tired. So very tired. The monster had chased him to his house and into his dreams. And now it had chased him out into the blizzard. . . .

So tired. He need to rest. He needed to sleep.

An elbow dug deep and painfully into his arm. "Wake up!" ordered Stacey. "You can't go to sleep. You might freeze to death or something."

"I'm not freezing to death," answered Kyle grouchily. "I'm warm, not freezing, thank you."

It was true, he realized. The combination of all his winter clothes, the blankets, and the heat from the other four bodies had been enough to keep him reasonably warm so far. He wasn't toasty warm and comfortable, but he wasn't freezing, either.

At least, not yet.

He looked at his watch. They'd been there an hour. He peered out from the edge of the sleeping bag. A layer of snow had already coated it. And it was getting dark.

Maria suddenly straightened up. "Did you hear that?" she asked.

"What?" Stacey leaned forward and cocked her head.

"That! That sound! It's the snowplows!" Maria flung the sleeping bag aside and sat up beside Kyle. "Quick. Get the flares so they don't hit us!"

She lunged for the flares just as Kyle lunged for her. He yanked her back down beneath the blankets.

"Shhh!" he said. "Be quiet."

"They're going to hit us!" cried Maria. "Kyle, let me go!"

"No. Be *quiet,*" Kyle ordered in a low, furious voice. His heart was pounding; his mouth was dry. His hands were shaking. "It's not the snowplows, Maria. It's not someone come to rescue us." He gave her arm a hard shake.

Maria said, her own voice lower now, "Well, then, what is it?"

Kyle took a deep breath. "Don't move. Don't anybody move. There's a monster out there. And it's looking for me."

CHAPTER
7

"Ha, ha, Kyle," said Maria. She reached for the flare. "You almost scared me."

"It's true," said Kyle desperately.

Jaws said, "What are you talking about?"

The wind howled and Kyle shivered. And then he felt it. A shudder, as if the ground under the car had moved.

"Shhhhh," he whispered.

Maria said, "That business about the snow monster was funny for a while, Kyle. I mean, the plastic shark teeth and all that were good. Really. But this is serious. *Serious*. Get it? We're trapped in a snowstorm."

Park spoke at last. He said slowly, "What makes you think there's a monster out there, Kyle?"

"Because I saw it."

"In your dreams," said Stacey sarcastically.

"That, too," said Kyle. Quickly he told the others what had happened the night before. "I thought it *was* a nightmare," he said. "Until I got to the school and saw what had happened. Then I realized that it wasn't the wind. There wasn't any wind last night. And I realized I hadn't been imagining things when I saw the monster's arms move. It's alive. The monster is alive, don't you see?''

"It can't be," said Maria. "That's crazy."

Stacey said, "How could something like that happen?"

The ground shook again. This time everyone felt it. Instinctively they all huddled closer together. Maria clutched the flare nervously. "It'll be dark soon," she said.

"Mom'll be back before then," said Kyle with a confidence he didn't feel. What if his mother didn't make it? Or what if there was no one home at Mr. King's? Or what if the rich snobs at the other end of the driveway said "Too bad. Let them eat snow"?

Or what if the monster . . .

No.

Kyle took a deep breath. "I think it's the eyeball," he said, answering Stacey's question. "I think it's the eyeball that did it."

"The marble one," said Park. "The one you think came from up on Graveyard Hill." He let out a very soft whistle. "That would do it."

"Wait a minute," said Maria. "You build this giant snowman and you call it a monster and you give it a marble eyeball from one of those statues up on Grave-

yard Hill? Are you crazy? That graveyard is . . . is . . ."
She paused, unable to think of a word. "Haunted" wasn't it. She wasn't sure there was a word that described exactly what effect Graveyard Hill was capable of having on anyone who came near it.

The ground shuddered again.

"Shh," said Kyle.

"Maybe we could melt it with the flares," whispered Maria.

The ground rocked again. The wind keened around the car.

Then it suddenly stopped. An awful stillness fell.

The hairs on the back of Kyle's neck stood up. He could sense his monster outside.

He wondered if his monster could sense him.

Maybe it's not after me, thought Kyle. *Maybe it just wants a friend.*

He had a sudden memory of the monster's evil expression, of the nasty sharp poke of its branch-claw hands.

He decided the friendship theory could wait.

They stayed still. Still as mice hunted by a cat. Trapped like mice in a mouse hole.

The ground shuddered. It shuddered again.

The car moved ever so slightly.

"It's here," gasped Maria. "It's found us."

"Shhh," said Stacey.

The car moved again.

Jaws, who'd been huddled in the corner, his mouth open, his eyes bulging, broke first.

"It's the monster!" he shrieked. "It's here! It's got us!"

"Jaws! Be quiet!" ordered Kyle. But it was too late. Jaws erupted from beneath the pile of sleeping bags and blankets into the frozen interior of the car.

"No! Jaws! Wait!" Stacey made a grab for Jaws, but she wasn't strong enough to hold him. Nobody could have. He was out of control. He flung Stacey to one side and pushed Kyle to the other. He dove for the handle of the car door and turned it.

It didn't move.

The car rocked again. In the growing darkness, Kyle thought he saw a black, clawlike hand skitter along the window.

He grabbed Jaws and pulled backward with all his might. Jaws's flailing arm caught him in the chest and knocked the wind out of him. Kyle fell back into Stacey and Park, and Jaws lunged once again for the door.

Hitting it with his shoulder, he forced it open and fell out into a wall of snow.

"Wait!" said Kyle hopelessly.

Jaws floundered to his feet. He dove into the wall of white snow like a swimmer and began to thrash forward.

A powerful roar engulfed them all. A huge blanket of

snow seemed to rise up and fall over Jaws. He disappeared from sight.

"*Aaaaaaaaaah! Noooooo!*" they heard him scream.

Kyle closed his eyes and waited for the worst to happen.

The wall of snow broke and fell around the car. A voice said, "I told you to stay in the car, Jaws Bennett! What on earth do you think you're doing?"

"Mom! Mom!" said Kyle.

"Shhh!" said Maria. "Maybe it's a trick. Maybe the monster just sounds like your mom."

"That's Mom," said Kyle. He dove out of the car and into the snow as incredibly bright lights pierced the gloom and the falling flakes. A huge roaring drowned out even the howl of the wind.

"The snowplow?" said Maria in a puzzled voice.

Holding Jaws tightly by the arm, Mrs. Chilton appeared in the beam of the powerful headlights. "Is everyone all right? No one else left the car, did they?"

"It wasn't a monster after all," said Maria.

"What?" said Kyle's mother.

"Nothing," said Maria quickly. She rolled her eyes at Kyle.

But Kyle didn't notice. He was looking around, trying to figure out where it was. He knew it was out there. He knew it wasn't very far away.

"Mr. King has his own snowplow," said Mrs. Chilton above the roar of the engine and the wind. "He just drove it down the driveway to the gate. There's only room for a couple of people in the cab of the plow. . . . Jaws, why don't you and Maria catch a ride with Mr. King? Kyle and Park and Stacey and I will hold on to the rope and follow. The road is clear enough so that we can't get lost. And of course, I'll hold on to the fence."

She paused. "Or we could wait for Mr. King to take the others back and return for us."

"No!" said Kyle quickly. He didn't want to wait around and take any chances. For some reason, the snowplow and all the people seemed to be keeping the monster at bay. But huddled in the back of the car, they were sitting ducks.

Mrs. Chilton nodded. "Okay. Here. We brought extra gloves and hats. They'll be drier and warmer for the walk up to the house. Take your other stuff off and leave it in the car, and we'll get going."

As Kyle pulled on the new gloves, he realized that he was beginning to get cold. Really cold.

He wondered if they could have lasted much longer in the car. He wondered whether the snowstorm would have gotten them if the monster hadn't.

He shook his head. No use thinking about that now. They were safe. All they had to do was make it up the long driveway to Mr. King's big, warm house.

After that he'd worry about monsters.

The snowplow turned, like a big, clumsy prehistoric animal, and went back through the huge gate. It crept up the driveway, its lights making a faint beam against the swirls of snow. It had made a road in the snow—a road that was almost a tunnel, so deep were the piles of snow it had pushed to either side.

"When we get to the driveway, we'll be out of the worst of the wind," said Mrs. Chilton. "The piles of snow on either side will protect us. It's like that all the way to the front steps."

She looped the rope around one hand and gave the end of it to Stacey, who looped the rope around her hand and passed it back to Park. Then Park took a loop and handed the rest of it to Kyle.

"Don't let go," said Mrs. Chilton. "And remember, just stay on the plowed part of the driveway."

The snowplow was almost out of sight now.

"Let's go," said Kyle's mother.

They plunged into the snow. As they went through the gate onto the driveway, Kyle looked back.

He saw a looming shape above the car. And then he saw the car turn sideways, like a toy being picked up by a little kid, and dive nosefirst into a snowdrift, and disappear.

• • •

The plowed road was icy and bumpy and slippery. Ahead of Kyle the rope jerked, and he was pulled forward. He raced up to find Park, on his hands and knees.

"Careful," said Kyle.

Park scrambled to his feet.

"Paaaark?" Stacey's voice blew back in the wind.

"Coming!" shouted Park.

But he didn't move. Instead he stopped, staring past Kyle's shoulder. The rope began to slide from his fingers.

"Careful!" said Kyle again, making a grab for the rope.

The ground tilted crazily under his feet.

The hair on his neck stood up, even under all the clothes he was wearing. He turned, too.

For an instant the snow stopped and the wind was still. For an instant he saw it.

The snow monster was standing there, just out of reach. It had grown. It was huge. Its stick arms protruded from enormous shoulders of ice. Its teeth were as long as icicles and looked as sharp as steak knives. Its eyes were red balls of fire. Somewhere along the way, it had acquired a row of buttons, probably from one of the other snowmen it had mangled at the schoolyard. The black top hat, ludicrously small now, was perched on its head once more. And around its neck was Park's red-and-white-striped scarf.

"Hey! That's my scarf!" said Park.

The monster opened its mouth. The teeth glistened.
It roared.

Park screamed, turned, and ran.

"Wait for me!" shouted Kyle, clinging desperately to the rope. He turned and ran after Park.

CHAPTER

8

The tunnel of snow seemed to stretch on forever. Kyle didn't know how long he'd slipped and skidded and scrambled forward. It was impossible to run more than two steps without falling.

The wind screamed past his ears. The snow blinded him. He couldn't hear. He couldn't see. He couldn't breathe.

He couldn't believe this was happening to him.

His feet went out from under him and he went straight up in the air and landed on his back. Had the monster pushed him? Made a grab for him and missed?

Quickly he rolled over and fought his way to his feet, his eyes scanning the snow and dark.

Nothing. Nothing but snow and more snow.

At least he'd remembered to keep the end of the rope looped around his hand. He turned and tightened his grip on the rope.

It stayed slack.

"Park?" said Kyle. He pulled on the rope. It didn't tighten. It didn't feel as if anybody was on the other end.

"Park, come on! This isn't funny!" shouted Kyle.

He gave the rope a good hard yank. "Park!"

The end of the rope popped up and flicked him in the face. Kyle yelped.

He rubbed his cheek. Then he realized what he was holding. He raised the end of the rope to eye level and squinted at it. The driving wind and snow brought cold tears to his eyes, and it was hard to see through the blur. He brought the rope closer.

He blinked. He was holding the end of the rope. And the end had been cut cleanly, as if by a knife or a pair of scissors.

Or a giant set of teeth.

"Paaaark!" screamed Kyle, starting forward. "Stacey! Mo-o-o-om!"

He slammed into something hard and cold. One of the walls in the tunnel of snow that led up to the house. He pushed off and spun around. It had gotten them. It had gotten all of them. He was the last one left, a stupid minnow on the end of a severed fishing line.

He turned and began to run.

How long had he clawed and scrambled along the tunnel before realizing that he didn't even know what direction he was going in?

He had no idea. The darkness was almost complete now. He wondered dimly if the snowplow had made it to the house. Would they come back and look for him? Would they find even a trace?

He turned and again crashed into a hard white wall of snow and ice.

He reached out to push away, and his hands encountered something hard and clawlike and bony.

He jerked back. He stood frozen for a long moment, his breath coming in painful rasps.

Then the clawlike hand swooped down out of the darkness and clamped on to his arm.

"No!" gasped Kyle. *"Noooooooooo!"*

He struggled wildly. But it was no use. The puny stick arms had acquired superhuman strength. Monster strength. They raised him up, up, up until he was high in the air, dangling helplessly, twisting in the blizzard wind.

Something red glowed near his face, like a live coal. In the freezing rush of wind, he felt the heat of it.

Then he was face-to-face with the monster.

"Put me down!" shouted Kyle, and kicked out at it. He didn't even come close.

The snow monster didn't move.

It stared at Kyle out of burning eyes. The heat of the eyes had melted the sockets a little, so that they were sunk deeply into the monster's face. Frozen tears from the melted snow tracked down the huge head.

"Let me go! Now!" ordered Kyle.

The monster gave no sign of having heard him.

Of course not, thought Kyle. *I forgot to give him ears*. The monster had a nose now, though. Somewhere along the way, it had acquired a carrot nose. Now that nose twitched, sniffing as if it smelled a delicious meal.

It was disgusting. Kyle would never be able to look at another carrot for the rest of his life.

His short life . . .

Kyle reached up and groped for the stick hand that was holding on to his jacket. *Maybe I can break off the fingers,* he thought. *Snap them like twigs.*

A breath of heat made him forget that plan. The monster had swung him closer. The eyes burned. Flames were dancing in them, dancing in the deep, sunken sockets. Then the monster smiled. The teeth dripped melting snow. Red melting snow.

Blood.

"Bloood!" screamed Kyle. It was true. The monster had eaten them. Eaten them all.

Tilting its head back and opening its mouth, the monster raised Kyle higher and higher. In another moment it would drop him into its mouth like a snack. Shred Kyle with those shark teeth. Grind him to bloody bits.

Hardly knowing what he was doing, Kyle fumbled with the zipper of his jacket. "Let go, let go, let go," he muttered.

The monster let go of Kyle's jacket.

Kyle ripped the zipper open and slid out of it.

The jacket fell into the monster's mouth. Kyle fell and bounced off the monster's chest and into an enormous drift of snow.

He floundered to his feet. He saw the monster's mouth open and close and open again.

Then the monster rolled its head on its round shoulders and roared.

It sounded like a Mack truck going through a tunnel.

It reached up with one black claw hand and ripped the shredded jacket out of its mouth and flung it down like an angry child. It rolled its head, and its eyes blazed furiously.

Kyle realized that the monster was looking for him. He had to get away.

He took off. Sinking up to his hips, scrambling on his hands and knees, he made his way across the frozen landscape. He was so afraid, he forgot to be cold. He was so afraid, he couldn't even think. He just ran.

He hit something hard and fell forward. Down. Down.

A well, thought Kyle wildly. *I've fallen down a well.*

But when he landed with a thump, he discovered that he'd fallen into some sort of covered feeding trough. The hay he'd landed on was almost soft. The snow had piled up around it, leaving an empty pocket below.

Kyle lay on the cold hay for a long time. He was out of the wind. He was out of the snow. It was very quiet.

He was very cold. He put his hands under his sweater. He began to shiver.

His teeth began to chatter. The chattering sounded loud in the sudden silence. For a moment he worried that the monster would hear him. Then he remembered that it had no ears.

It has teeth, though, Kyle thought. *It totally pulped my jacket.*

He took a deep breath. He wasn't as winded as he had been. The unexpected rest had helped. He began to feel a little more hopeful. He had eluded the monster this long. Maybe he could escape. Maybe he could find the house and get inside to safety.

Kyle sat up.

And the roof of his snow shelter caved in as if it had been hit by an avalanche.

CHAPTER
9

Kyle didn't even have time to scream. He ducked and covered his head, trying to roll out of the way.

Huge clawed hands reached down, opening and closing hungrily.

Sniff, sniff, *sniff*. Even in the avalanche of snow, Kyle could hear it sniffing.

He rolled under the trough, and his back hit something solid. The claws swept past, and he shrank back. He groped behind him.

Wood. Kyle turned over and saw that the trough wasn't just a covered feeding trough in the middle of a pasture. It was a feeding trough next to a building. A building made of red boards.

A barn.

A long, bony finger curled almost delicately under the trough. It touched Kyle's foot and paused.

Kyle didn't wait. He lunged out from under the trough at the far end, headfirst into a wall of drifted snow. He fought his way upward, reaching out to make sure that he was staying next to the barn.

Snow filled his eyes and mouth. It burned his tongue.

And then he was breathing icy air again. This time the burning was sweet. He took a deep breath.

And the snow monster roared behind him.

Kyle jumped forward and fell. He felt the snow shift like pudding beneath him. A clawlike hand brushed over him. He leaped forward again onto his hands and knees.

Dimly, to one side, he could see the huge barn now, a darker shape in the gathering twilight, its bulk standing out against the driving snow. He scrambled around it.

The door. The door. He had to find the door. . . .

A hand grabbed his ankle. Kyle reached back and bent one of the twig fingers back as hard as he could.

It didn't snap, but the monster let go and let out a roar of pain.

Great, thought Kyle. *Now he's really angry.* He reached the corner and pulled himself around it.

Nothing. No door. The back of the barn. But there was less snow here. Kyle got to his feet and sprinted forward.

Then he saw it. Lights. Even in the blinding snow, bright lights, a whole buildingful.

People. Safety. If only he could get there.

But there was a huge expanse of unbroken snow between Kyle and those lights. How could he out-run—?

It grabbed his head.

His hat came off.

Kyle didn't wait. He jumped away from the barn and started to run.

For the first two steps, the snow's hard-packed surface held. Then he sank through. He stopped. He realized that his jumping and running were what was making the snow give way so easily. If he could force himself to walk slowly, it wouldn't break so much. He wouldn't sink so deep.

It wouldn't feel like it, but he would move faster.

He took a giant, slow step forward. His foot sank, but only to the ankle. He took another giant step.

Behind him the monster pushed forward like a huge monster snowplow.

Kyle took another giant step. And another, keeping his eyes on the glow of light that shined through the blizzard.

A wall of snow hit him from behind.

He fell forward.

He rolled to one side instinctively as the monster hand came down. Huge teeth gnashed in the air above him.

Kyle took off one glove and threw it up into the monster's gaping, dripping mouth.

The monster fell back, chewing.

Scrambling to his feet, Kyle began to giant-step forward again.

He made it three more steps when the monster struck again.

This time Kyle didn't fall. He dodged, hurling his other glove up at the monster.

He didn't wait for the monster to start chewing. He walked forward.

There. There. He was almost there.

The monster grabbed his foot. Kicking, falling, Kyle pulled off his scarf and threw it toward the monster.

Like a big cat, the monster reached out and grabbed the scarf as the wind whipped it into the air.

It let go of Kyle.

Kyle forgot about walking slowly. The last encounter had broken his nerve. He lunged forward, fought forward, flailed with all his might.

And then he was there. He'd reached the light.

He was pressed against a sheet of glass. It was a building made of glass that was coated with frost.

Kyle raised his hand and hit the glass.

His hand bounced back.

He scraped at the frost. "Help!" he screamed. "Somebody help me!"

His words blew away.

Somehow he managed to clear a small patch on the glass.

He was looking down into blue water. A pool. A huge swimming pool. Deck chairs were scattered around it. A float shaped like a plastic gorilla bobbed gently on the surface of the water. Little wisps of steam rose up from the pool and curled invitingly upward.

For a moment Kyle thought he was imagining things. The monster chase had driven him out of his wits.

Then he realized that it really was a swimming pool. A heated swimming pool. The drifts of snow were so high that he was almost on the roof, looking down into it.

"Help!" he shrieked. *"Heeelp!"*

The claws closed around his shoulders. Kyle struck the glass again. "Help me!" he cried. He was being lifted up. He kicked at the glass as he rose.

He was so close. So close. And now he was going to get eaten alive.

He spun around and raised his arms and slipped out of his sweater like a banana out of a peel.

He fell onto the domed roof of the glass poolhouse.

This time he felt the glass give under the impact of his falling body. He began to slide off, and reached out desperately to save himself. His fingers hooked under the edges of one of the panes.

He didn't know how long he had hung there by his fingers before he felt the glass poolhouse shake with the impact of the monster.

He rolled carefully over.

It was leaning over the poolhouse, its eyes blazing bloody red, its teeth gnashing and clashing. Bits of wool from Kyle's sweater clung to the teeth like gruesome floss.

Moving carefully, clinging for his life, Kyle pulled himself a little farther up on the roof.

A little farther. A little farther still. Just out of the monster's reach.

If I could jump up and down, I might break the glass, thought Kyle. *I could fall into the pool. . . .*

But he didn't have the strength. It took all the energy he had left just to cling there.

He was going to be a frozen dinner after all.

The poolhouse shuddered. The claws scrabbled over the glass.

Kyle looked down at the warm blue water.

He looked back at the monster.

He rolled onto his side and hooked the fingers of one hand as tightly as he could onto the edge of the

pane of glass. He raised the other hand and waved reck-
lessly. Defiantly. Insanely.

He began to laugh.

"Come and get me, you big, stupid monster! Come
and get me!" he shouted.

CHAPTER
10

The monster lunged. Kyle drew his legs up.

The hands touched his feet. He was being pulled into the air. The monster was on the roof. It raised Kyle feetfirst into the air. It opened its mouth.

The roof gave way. It shattered into a million pieces of glass.

I hope this is safety glass, Kyle had time to think.

Then he was falling through the air. He hit the water with a splash. He was sinking. He tried to swim upward. He swallowed a mouthful of water. His hand hit something, and he held on.

Then everything went dark.

"Kyle? Kyle! Speak to me! Oh, Kyle, are you all right?"

Kyle frowned. "Mom?" he said, and choked on a mouthful of water.

"Kyle!" It was his mother. She grabbed him and gave him a big kiss.

Kyle was too tired to fight it. He let her. For a minute.

Another voice, a stranger's voice, said, "Looks like he's gonna be all right. Lucky that was safety glass. But I've got a bone to pick with that construction company. That glass is supposed to be able to support much more weight. So it doesn't cave in when we have snow like this, you know?"

Kyle opened his eyes. He was lying on a wicker lounge chair inside a small room filled with plants and other wicker furniture. The room had a glass sliding door that opened out onto the pool. The sliding door was closed.

Snow was falling on the pool and melting as it fell.

The room was full of people. Park, Stacey, Maria, Jaws, Mrs. Chilton, and a man Kyle didn't recognize were all crowded into it, looking down at Kyle.

Kyle's mother regained control of herself and sat back. "We were so worried about you," she said.

Mr. King, a large man in a bright blue ski suit, said, "Took my snowplow back out to look for you. Then we heard the crash and the alarm went off."

"It was awesome," said Stacey. "I mean, the whole roof caved in and the alarm went ape."

"Why did you let go of the rope?" asked Mrs. Chilton almost angrily.

88

"I . . . fell," said Kyle.

"You are one lucky young man, do you know that?" said Mr. King.

Maria said, "Did the snowman—Owww!"

Stacey had stepped on her foot.

Kyle said quickly, "I'm cold."

Mr. King laughed. "I just bet you are, young man. Let's get you out of those clothes and into some dry ones. I have some that might fit, from when my own sons were growing up. We were just making some hot chocolate when the roof went. . . . You'll want some of that, too."

He led the way out of the room.

Kyle got up shakily. "Can you walk?" asked his mother anxiously.

"Mom," said Kyle, embarrassed.

He stood up. The room spun around.

Park grabbed one arm. "Gotcha," he said.

Leaning on Park more than he cared to admit, Kyle allowed himself to be led out of the room.

"What I don't understand," Mr. King was saying, "was how you got up on the roof in the first place. I didn't realize the drifts had gotten so high. Must have happened today."

"Kyle, where are the rest of your clothes?" asked Maria.

Park said, "They probably fell off when you fell in the pool."

"Yeah," said Kyle. "That's it."

"Your sweater, too?" asked Maria.

"It was pulling me under, so I took it off," said Kyle.

Mr. King pushed a door open. "My oldest son's old room. Bathroom to the left. Clothes in the drawers. Get dry and warm and come on down for hot chocolate. Park here'll show you the way."

"Do you want me to—" Mrs. Chilton began.

"I'm fine, Mom," said Kyle quickly.

Mrs. Chilton smiled. "Well, you're beginning to sound like yourself again, so I guess you're okay."

Park and Kyle went into the bedroom. "Coming?" Park asked Jaws.

"Hot chocolate," said Jaws briefly, shaking his head.

Jaws and Stacey and Maria left with Mr. King and Mrs. Chilton. Park closed the door behind them.

He turned to Kyle.

"The rope had been cut in half," he said. "I didn't realize you weren't there until we got to the house. Then I saw the rope and I thought the monster had gotten you."

"It was the monster, wasn't it?"

Kyle began to pull clothes out of the drawers. He found a pair of jeans and a sweater. Thick socks. Underwear. He even found a pair of old sneakers in the closet that looked as if they'd fit.

"Wow!" said Kyle, momentarily distracted. "These sneakers aren't bad."

Park gestured impatiently. "Mr. King has tons of stuff. He's already given us tons of dry clothes. He's saved all the clothes that used to belong to his kids. You wouldn't think a rich guy would do that, would you? When I'm rich, I'm not even going to wash my dirty clothes. I'm just going to give them away."

"Like Polly?" asked Kyle slyly.

"That was low," said Park. "So. It was the monster. Right?"

"Yeah," Kyle said. "It was. But don't let it get around, okay? I just got lost."

Park nodded. "I know. But I saw it, you know. I knew it was real all along. The minute you told me about using that eyeball, I knew."

Somehow Kyle wasn't surprised. After all, Park had had at least one encounter with weirdness at Graveyard School himself.

He said, "Yeah. It was the eyeball that did it."

He went into the bathroom and began to run hot water into the tub. It swirled around and around. Steam rose up.

Beautiful hot water. Wonderful steam.

Kyle said, "It chased me. I kept throwing things at it as decoys—gloves, shoes, like that."

"Wow!" said Park admiringly. "Good thinking."

"Yeah," said Kyle. Now that he had time to think, he realized it had been pretty good thinking.

"Anyway, it chased me to the pool. It grabbed me. I fed it my sweater, and it dropped me onto the roof. I thought it had me then. Until I realized I was looking down at a heated pool."

Park said, "You are a true genius, Kyle."

"Lucky," said Kyle. He gathered up all the clothes and took them back into the bathroom, dropping them in a heap on the floor. He found a towel. The whole bathroom was filling up with steam.

"So I told the monster to come and get me," said Kyle. "And it did. I thought for a minute my plan wouldn't work. It was about to put my feet in its mouth when the whole roof gave way. We fell into the pool."

"And the monster *melted*. Great. Outstanding!" said Park.

"After that, I don't know what happened," said Kyle.

Park said, "We'd just handed all our clothes over to Mr. King's housekeeper so she could wash and dry them. Your mom and Mr. King were out in the snow-plow. Everyone kept asking me what happened to you, and Maria kept saying, 'It's the monster, it's the monster.' I think the housekeeper thought she'd lost her mind out in the storm. Then Mrs. King came in and told us she was going to fix us hot chocolate.

And that's when the alarm went off and we heard this gigantic crash. And a roar like a tornado or something."

"I'd just fallen in the pool, I guess," said Kyle.

"I guess so! We got there and the whole glass roof had caved in and the snow was falling and there were big chunks of snow in the pool, and the pool looked like it was boiling! I mean, it was hissing, and the chunks were crashing into the walls and surfing around the pool like they were alive!" Park's voice was enthusiastic, but Kyle shuddered.

The monster had been melting. Boiling away in the hot water—like that experiment they'd done in science where they'd left a tooth in a bottle of cola and the cola had eaten the tooth away. Only that had taken much longer. This had been over in minutes.

Kyle shuddered again, imagining it.

"Then we saw you, floating in the middle of the pool, holding on to this gorilla float."

"The gorilla float?" For a moment Kyle had forgotten about the float. Then he remembered and nodded. "Oh, yeah. I saw it when I was up on the roof. Lucky it was there."

"Mr. King and your mom drove up in the snowplow about then and came running in just as Stacey and I hauled you out of the pool. They took you into the sunroom off the pool and you woke up."

"Wow!" said Kyle. He glanced at Park. "Thanks for pulling me out of the pool."

"Don't thank me," said Park. "I wouldn't have missed it for anything!"

The hot chocolate was delicious. Kyle sipped it slowly.

He peered out across the frozen landscape.

It wasn't as frozen as it had once been. In fact, it was looking distinctly blurry around the edges.

The long, hard winter was over. The season of the killer blizzards and record snowfalls had ended. The thirteen-snowstorm winter had passed.

Spring was in the air.

"I don't get it," whined Polly. "Why would Mr. King donate hot chocolate to Graveyard School? If you'd crashed into my swimming pool and broken the roof, I would have sued you."

Kyle shrugged. He couldn't explain it, either. But Mr. King had turned out to be a nice guy. And the hot chocolate he'd donated to Graveyard School— with instructions for everyone who wanted a cup to be given one every day after school for the rest of the winter before going out into the snow—had suited Kyle just fine.

He looked up and caught Park's eye. Park raised his cup and grinned.

Maria and Stacey grinned, too.

Jaws didn't notice. He was staring longingly at the huge dispenser of hot chocolate, clearly trying to figure out how he could get a second cup.

But he wouldn't ask. Because it was Dr. Morthouse herself who was handing out the hot chocolate. Kyle figured she thought it made her look good to the parents as they drove up to the school. Or maybe she wanted to make sure no one got seconds.

Who knew? But her smile was enough to freeze the hot chocolate.

"We're lucky we're not all dead," said Polly.

"You got home safely in that blizzard, no prob," said Maria. "What are you complaining about?"

Polly ignored her. She switched her attention back to Kyle. "And how come you got all those new clothes? A new parka! New gloves! A new hat and boots, too!"

Kyle said, "I told you, Polly. I lost them when I got lost in the snow. And the rest got ruined in the pool."

"Huh? You shouldn't have gotten lost. I don't see why you should be rewarded for it."

Park adjusted his red-and-white-striped scarf. The dunking in the pool had shrunk it a little, but it still fit. And no way was Park going to part with a scarf that had been worn by a monster.

Mr. King had been puzzled by the carrot, the buttons, the top hat, and the set of plastic shark teeth that had turned up in the pool and in the pool filter. "Must've been blown in by the storm," he finally concluded.

"Drink your hot chocolate, Polly," said Stacey.

"Or I'll drink it," volunteered Jaws.

Polly glared at them and quickly began to drink her hot chocolate.

"Da, da, da da *da*." The opening bars of "Row, Row, Row Your Boat." Kyle sighed and pitched his empty hot-chocolate cup into the recycling bin.

Some things never changed. His mother had given Mr. King a lifetime of free towing in gratitude for saving them. She had also repaired the Chilton family car—giving it a new horn.

"That's our ride," said Stacey, finishing her own chocolate.

They went down the steps.

At the bottom Kyle stopped and looked back. The little kids had started building snowmen as soon as the blizzard was over. When they'd seen that the storm had completely wiped out Kyle's snow monster, they'd seemed satisfied that justice had been done.

Kyle hadn't built a new snowman. He didn't think he ever would. He'd had enough snow to last him a lifetime.

Maybe his future would be in swimming pools.

He pushed his hands deeper into his pockets as he turned to climb into the car.

His fingers touched something cold. He traced the outline of a marble eyeball and smiled to himself.

And maybe his future wouldn't be in swimming pools after all.

Who knew what the future held?

Anything could happen.

Create your own monster!

Take a die from a board game and roll it four times. Write down each number you roll, in order. The first number you roll will correspond to the Head list below. The second will correspond to the Body list, the third to the Arms, and the fourth to the Legs. When you've matched each number with a body part, turn the page and draw the dastardly creature. Then start over to make more monster fun!

Example:
You roll 3, 5, 2, and 1.
You have rolled a monster with a huge eyeball for a head, a shark's body, lizard arms, and mermaid fin legs!

Head:
1. Vampire's head
2. A clump of worms
3. A huge eyeball
4. Werewolf's head
5. Crocodile's head
6. Rat's head

Body:
1. Snake
2. Human
3. Horse
4. Robot
5. Shark
6. Tree trunk

Arms:
1. Carrots
2. Lizard
3. Brooms
4. Knives
5. Tree branches
6. Cat paws

Legs:
1. Mermaid fins
2. Goat legs
3. String beans
4. Metal springs
5. Wheels
6. Scissors

Draw your monster here:

99

TILL YOU

With each and every one of these scary, creepy, delightfully, frightfully funny books, you'll be dying to go to the *Graveyard School!*

Order any or all of the books in this scary new series by **Tom B. Stone**! Just check off the titles you want, then fill out and mail the order form below.

☐ 0-553-48223-8	**DON'T EAT THE MYSTERY MEAT!**	$3.50/$4.50 Can.
☐ 0-553-48224-6	**THE SKELETON ON THE SKATEBOARD**	$3.50/$4.50 Can.
☐ 0-553-48225-4	**THE HEADLESS BICYCLE RIDER**	$3.50/$4.50 Can.
☐ 0-553-48226-2	**LITTLE PET WEREWOLF**	$3.50/$4.50 Can.
☐ 0-553-48227-0	**REVENGE OF THE DINOSAURS**	$3.50/$4.50 Can.

Bantam Doubleday Dell
Books For Young Readers

BDD BOOKS FOR YOUNG READERS
2451 South Wolf Road
Des Plaines, IL 60018

Please send me the items I have checked above. I am enclosing $_____
(please add $2.50 to cover postage and handling).
Send check or money order, no cash or C.O.D.s please.

NAME _____

ADDRESS _____

CITY _____ STATE _____ ZIP _____

Please allow four to six weeks for delivery.
Prices and availability subject to change without notice.   BFYR 113 2/95

CHART YOUR COURSE TO EXCITEMENT!

Take the journey of a lifetime with *Gary Paulsen World of Adventure!* Every story is a thrilling, action-packed odyssey, containing an adventure guide with important survival tips no camper or adventurer should be without!

Order any or all of these exciting **Gary Paulsen** adventures. Just check off the titles you want, then fill out and mail the order form below.

☐ 0-440-41023-1	**LEGEND OF RED HORSE CAVERN**	$3.50/$4.50 Can.
☐ 0-440-41024-X	**RODOMONTE'S REVENGE**	$3.50/$4.50 Can.
☐ 0-440-41025-8	**ESCAPE FROM FIRE MOUNTAIN**	$3.50/$4.50 Can.
☐ 0-440-41026-6	**THE ROCK JOCKEYS**	$3.50/$4.50 Can.

Bantam Doubleday Dell
Books For Young Readers

BDD BOOKS FOR YOUNG READERS
2451 South Wolf Road
Des Plaines, IL 60018

Please send me the items I have checked above. I am enclosing $_____
(please add $2.50 to cover postage and handling).
Send check or money order, no cash or C.O.D.s please.

NAME_____

ADDRESS_____

CITY_____STATE_____ZIP_____

Please allow four to six weeks for delivery.
Prices and availability subject to change without notice.   BFYR 115 3/95

THE SADDLE CLUB™